THIS WALKER BOOK BELONGS TO:

_____

_____

_____

For Lauren, Allison and Amanda, the best fish feeders in Texas.
And for Sarah, in honour of her goldfish, Lucky.

K. B.

For Diane.
N. Z. J.

First published 2005 by Walker Books Ltd
87 Vauxhall Walk, London SE11 5HJ

2 4 6 8 10 9 7 5 3 1

Text © 2005 Kelly Bennett
Illustrations © 2005 Noah Z. Jones

The right of Kelly Bennett and Noah Z. Jones to be identified as author
and illustrator respectively of this work has been asserted by them in
accordance with the Copyright, Designs and Patents Act 1988

This book has been typeset in Shinn Medium

Printed in Singapore

British Library Cataloguing in Publication Data:
a catalogue record for this book is available from the British Library

ISBN 1-84428-288-0

www.walkerbooks.co.uk

NOT NORMAN

A Goldfish Story

Kelly Bennett

illustrated by **Noah Z. Jones**

WALKER BOOKS
AND SUBSIDIARIES
LONDON • BOSTON • SYDNEY • AUCKLAND

Your Fish
and You

When I was given Norman, I didn't want to keep him.
I wanted a different kind of pet.

Not Norman.

I wanted a pet who could run and catch.
Or one who could climb trees and chase a ball of string.
A soft, furry pet to sleep on my bed at night.
Not Norman.

All Norman does is swim around and around and around and around
and around and around and around and around...

"That's it, Norman," I decide.
"I'm swapping you for a good pet."
Norman doesn't move. Not even a fin twitches.

How can I swap him like this?
No one will want a sorry-looking fish in a gunky bowl.

When I drop Norman into his nice, clean bowl, he starts dipping and flipping, flapping his fins around. He looks so silly I have to laugh.

"Don't think that just because you made me laugh, I'm going to keep you," I tell him. "Tomorrow you're going."

Norman blows a stream of bubbles.

The next day I take Norman to school with me.
I plan to talk someone, anyone,
into taking him.

On the way there, we see my friend Will.
Will has a really great dog – and seven puppies.
"How about swapping one of your pups for Norman?" I ask.
"Who's Norman?" asks Will.
"My goldfish," I say.

By the time I rescue Norman, half his water is gone!

"I'm sorry," I tell Norman when we get to school. "I'm really sorry."
He just stares at me all googly-eyed.

After break, I get a chance to speak to the class.
Just as I start to talk about goldfish, Emily shouts,
"Izzy's gone! Who let my snake loose?"

Does anyone hear the story of how I got Norman?
Does anyone even ask to hold his bowl? No.
They're all jumping and screaming and chasing the snake.
Not Norman. He's looking right at me.

"Thanks for listening," I tell him.

That afternoon we go to my music lesson.
As soon as it's over, I'm taking Norman back to the pet shop.

I take out my tuba and begin to play.

Bom bom bo

I glance over at Norman. He's swaying back and forth.
Glu glu glu glug, he mouths.

"Look! Norman's singing," I say.
"Pay attention!" snaps Mr Baker. "And *try* to play the right notes."

aaaa Ba ba ba boooo Bo bo bo beeee.

Mr Baker makes me stay for extra practice.
By the time my lesson is over,
it's too late to go to the pet shop.
"Don't think that just because you like my music,
I'm going to keep you," I tell Norman.

He glugs.

That night I'm sound asleep when ...

SCREECH, SCRITCH!

What's that noise?

SCRATCH SCRITCH SCREEEECH!

Yikes, there's something at the window!

Then, out of the corner of my eye,

I spot ...

Norman!

He isn't scared.

He isn't swimming around in circles either.

He glugs and gives me a little wave.

I'm not alone.

Together, Norman and I slide open the curtains.
It was just a broken tree branch scratching the window.

"Thanks for watching out for me," I tell Norman.

On Saturday I take Norman to the pet shop, just like I said I would. I look at the cats and dogs and snakes and birds. I look at the hamsters and mice and lizards too.

They all look like good pets,
but they are ...

NOT NORMAN.

When I was given Norman, I wasn't sure I wanted to keep him.
But now, even if I could pick any pet
in the whole world, I wouldn't swap him.

Not Norman.

WALKER BOOKS is the world's leading
independent publisher of children's books.
Working with the best authors and illustrators
we create books for all ages, from babies
to teenagers – books your child will
grow up with and always remember. So…

FOR THE BEST CHILDREN'S BOOKS,
LOOK FOR THE BEAR